OLD WINTER

OLD WINTER

JUDITH BENÉT RICHARDSON

PICTURES BY R. W. ALLEY

ORCHARD BOOKS
NEW YORK

For James, Sara Rose, and William Benét
—J.B.R.

For Zoë, younger than springtime
—R.W.A.

Orchard Books, 95 Madison Avenue, New York, NY 10016

The text of this book is set in 13 point Bookman.
The illustrations are pen-and-ink drawings with watercolors.
Manufactured in the United States of America. Printed by Barton Press, Inc.
Bound by Horowitz/Rae. Book design by Sylvia Frezzolini Severance.

10 9 8 7 6 5 4 3 2 1

Library of Congress Cataloging-in-Publication Data
Richardson, Judith Benét. date.
Old winter / story by Judith Benét Richardson ; pictures by R. W. Alley.
p. cm.
Summary: When the townspeople complain about the cold weather,
Old Winter's feelings are hurt and he takes a very long nap in the
meat locker of the P&J Supermarket.
ISBN 0-531-09533-9. — ISBN 0-531-08883-9 (lib. bdg.)
[1. Winter—Fiction. 2. Spring—Fiction. 3. Gratitude—Fiction.]
I. Alley, R. W. (Robert W.), ill. II. Title.
PZ7.R394901 1996 [E]—dc20 96-85

Old Winter was in the P & J Supermarket, rummaging through the ice-cream freezer. He couldn't decide whether he wanted Brazil-nut crunch ice cream or a chocolate-covered frozen banana for dinner. I'd better eat a good meal, he thought, because tonight—I fly south!

"I *hate* winter," said Mrs. Ferguson.
"All this dirty snow, all these heavy clothes!
Car trouble. Ice on the sidewalk. I'm fed up."

Old Winter peered
around the end of the
aisle. Is that me she
is talking about? he
wondered.

"This rotten winter! It's the worst! I'll sure be glad when I can stop shoveling snow and get out in the garden," bellowed Bob Bailey.

"And play baseball," said his son Peter. "The heck with old winter!" He tried to slide into home plate but his boots stuck to the linoleum.

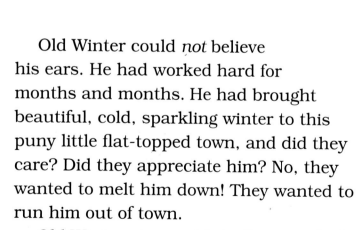

Old Winter could *not* believe
his ears. He had worked hard for
months and months. He had brought
beautiful, cold, sparkling winter to this
puny little flat-topped town, and did they
care? Did they appreciate him? No, they
wanted to melt him down! They wanted to
run him out of town.

Old Winter stomped into the meat locker.
He slammed the door and slumped down in the dark
corner where he kept his special boots, his wind whistle,
and his snowflakes.

"They'll probably hate me
in South America, too,"
he grumbled. "I'm not doing
one more thing for *anyone*.
So there."

Old Winter lay down and went to sleep. And while he slept,
for miles and miles around him, cold winter covered the land.

It was the longest winter the townspeople could remember. Icicles hung down to the ground and snow piled up to the rooftops. Peter Bailey's pitching arm grew weak. Mrs. Ferguson slept in her tam-o'-shanter and her matching long underwear.

Two months later, Winter woke up and yawned and stretched. He shuffled out of the meat locker and made his way to the front door of the P & J.

The world looked even worse. The snow was packed and filthy. Cars were crusted over with mud and salt, except for two clear half circles on each windshield.

A few people in thick coats
huddled by the newspaper box.
Old Winter could see the headline:
TOWN FROZEN:
IS THERE NO END IN SIGHT?

"Squawk, squawk! There he is, there he is!" Old Winter looked around to see four bedraggled Canada geese waddling toward him. Their white neck feathers were dirty and their long gray wings dragged in the slushy snow.

"Hissssssss, hisssssss." The geese stuck out their necks at Old Winter.

"What's the matter with *you*?" said Old Winter crossly, but he edged away from their beaks.

"We are desssperate," said the most tattered of the Canada geese. "There's nothing to eat here as long as you're around!"

"Get to the point," growled Old Winter.

"We beg you, sssir, to pleassse, pleassse take your leave the way you alwaysss have done."

"I'll go when I'm good and ready," said Old Winter.
He stared at the geese with his fierce gray eyes. Their wings drooped and they turned away.

Suddenly Winter noticed
a woman dressed in a bright
green T-shirt get out of a
shiny yellow car.
"No, don't come out yet,"
she said to the two children
still in the backseat.
"No, Daff. You'll freeze,
Violet. Stay put, and I'll see
if I can find out."

She looked around and saw Old Winter. "Oh, there you are!"
she said in surprise. "You're usually gone by the time I get here.
Is anything wrong? Is there anything I can do to help?"

When he didn't answer, she asked softly,
"Did you get tired? Too tired to go on?"

Old Winter shuffled his feet. He looked
down and noticed a few snowdrops that
had broken the dirty crust of ice.
He thought of all the other
bulbs planted underground,
waiting to push through.
He looked at the geese
standing miserably by
a frozen puddle.

Daff rolled down the car window. "Time to go," she called. "It's our turn!"

"I was just leaving," grumbled the old man. "Don't rush me."

"Well," said Spring, "I happen to know they're longing for you in Chile. The plants are getting worn out from flowering so much, and those spectacled bears will be grumpy if they don't get their long winter's sleep. The world needs us, Old Winter, and we've just got to keep going whether we like it or not!"

Winter remembered how much he liked to visit South America, and how exciting it was to scatter the first few snowflakes over the pampas.

He ran back to the meat locker to get his boots. He picked up his bag of snowflakes and his wind whistle.

With one mighty stride, he was out of the
parking lot and on his way.

"So long," called Daff, as he bounded over her
head. Old Winter waved back with a blast of sleet.
Daff jumped behind the car.

The Canada geese looked up, startled.
"Hink? Hink? Hink?" questioned one of the geese.

"A-honk! A-honk!" called another.

All over town, people looked up. A warm breeze
wafted over the parking lot. An icicle fell with a
crash off the side of the P&J.

And then it rained.

After three days, the sun shone out from behind a cloud. "Play ball!" cheered Peter. "No more boots! Hurray for cleats!" He practiced his swing so hard that he fell in a puddle.

"Yes, spring is finally here," whined Mrs. Ferguson. "And so is the mud! My driveway is a swamp."

"Washed away all my topsoil in one night, dag nab it!" said Bob Bailey.

"Some people are never happy," said Daff.

"You can't grow anything without a little rain," said Violet.

Spring took some seed packages from the rack just inside the open door of the P & J.

"What are you going to plant?" asked Bob.

"Oh, a little bit of everything," she answered.

She winked at the Baileys and headed for the door.

Then Spring drove off to the north,
scattering seeds in every direction.

And far away in Argentina, the first snowflake drifted down onto the feathery grass of the pampas.